ABOUT

First cultivated in an[cient times, honey—]
vitamin rich, king am[ong foods—has reigned supreme in]
nutrition. Its story is told and its life-giving secrets proclaimed in this book.

By the same author:
ABOUT AROMATIC HERBS
ABOUT COMFREY
ABOUT GARLIC
ABOUT POLLEN

MUSHROOMS
ORGANIC GARDENING AND FARMING

With Alan Moyle:
ABOUT KELP

ABOUT SOYA BEANS

Wonder Source of Protein and Energy

by
G. J. BINDING
M.B.E.

THORSONS PUBLISHERS LIMITED
Wellingborough, Northamptonshire

First published 1970
Second Impression 1971
Third Impression 1977
Second Edition, revised and
reset 1980

© G. J. BINDING 1980

This book is sold subject to the condition that it shall not, by way of trade or otherwise, be lent, re-sold, hired out, or otherwise circulated without he publisher's prior consent in any form of binding or cover other than that in which it is published and without a similar condition including this condition being imposed on the subsequent purchaser.

ISBN 0 7225 0644 9

Printed and bound in Great Britain by
Hunt Barnard Printing Ltd.,
Aylesbury, Bucks

CONTENTS

Chapter		Page
1.	Beans in General	7
2.	History of the Soya Bean	13
3.	Content of Soya Beans	19
4.	About Lecithin – Vital for Retaining Youth	28
5.	The Soya Bean in the Far East	33
6.	American Influence on the Soya Bean	37
7.	Industrial Uses in America	45
8.	The Soya Bean and World Food Shortage	47
9.	Soya Bean Recipes	57

ACKNOWLEDGEMENTS

I wish to express my sincere thanks to Messrs. S. Puspalm, K. Menon, John Pang, Haji Sulieman, and other friends (and their families) in the Far East, through whose hospitality my family and I first encountered the soya bean in its many forms.

I also wish to thank:

The President, Soybean Council of America, Washington D.C., U.S.A.

The Editor, The Soybean Digest, Hudson, Iowa, U.S.A.

Worthington Soy Foods Inc., Worthington, Ohio, U.S.A.

CHAPTER ONE

BEANS IN GENERAL

The bean, one of the oldest vegetables known to man, has always been surrounded by strange stories, legends and sayings. We are all familiar with that lovable character Jack and The Beanstalk, and such expressions as 'Full of beans'. Having a good time was often referred to as a 'Beanfeast' or 'Beano'. The person who presided as King over the Twelfth Night Festivities was named the 'Bean King'. He gained this honour by getting the bean buried in the Twelfth Night Cake.

Types of Beans

There is hardly another vegetable which produces so many different varieties, colours and shapes as the bean. World wide there are no less than 150 species of endless strains and every hue of the rainbow. Beans have always been recognized as delicious, appetizing and wholesome, full of body-building goodness. One cannot obtain a finer vegetable than freshly gathered beans cooked and served straight from the garden. I have never met anyone, young or old, who does not like at least one kind of bean.

This vital food is taken so much for granted. During winter months when crops cannot be grown, frozen beans are available and a wide choice of tinned kinds to satisfy all tastes. For those who dislike frozen or canned foods there are numerous dried beans until fresh vegetables are again in season. So at all times beans can be obtained to provide meals; from bacon and beans at breakfast, an odd snack of beans on toast, or as a fine health giving supplement to other vegetables at a main meal.

Folklore

Beans play a conspicuous part in the folklore of England and many other countries. In Yorkshire, even today, some believe that sleeping in the beanfields will produce vivid dreams. Miners, in many places still believe that accidents in pits are more likely to occur when beans are in flower. Heathen peoples always considered that plants with strong smelling flowers, especially the bean, were closely related to ghosts and the deceased. A Roman festival took place on the first day of June in which beans were offered to the dead.

An ancient Aryan traditional religious belief was that beans and honey were held to be sacred food to be offered to the departed. This little seed was also used in a form of balloting by the Romans and Greeks when a white bean signified Yes and a black one No. In Italy until about 50 years ago it was the custom to distribute beans to the poor on All Souls Day. A Josh Billings was impressed by the fact that one quart of beans on being boiled for two hours came out as one and a half gallons. A very strange account was written by Pliny, the Naturalist, that man would emerge from manure heaps if beans were planted within them.

The Soya Bean

So much may be said about beans available to man today, what he thinks about them now, and the strange beliefs and customs surrounding this vegetable in an age gone by. However, one little specimen of the bean family, conspicuous by its absence as part of the diet of the average English Family, is the soya bean. This is to be deplored, and to say the least is unfortunate.

Prior to the second world war England was one of the world's largest importers of the soya bean. This state of affairs no longer exists today. The decline in popularity of this vegetable, in England and on the Continent, may be influenced by the fact that the crop cannot be successfully cultivated in Europe. Furthermore, people today in times of fuller employment and greater prosperity seek more expensive processed foods, rather than natural health giving vegetables. As a result a fine nutritious food which gives 100% value for money, and is cheap enough to be within the reach of all, is lost.

More Value for Money

Josh Billings, the character out of folklore, claimed that one quart of beans became one and a half gallons on boiling for two hours. This, to say the least, is a great exaggeration. However, from my own vast experience of the soya bean, one pint, will produce a considerable supplement, ideal if served in small quantities together with other vegetables.

Like the procedure reported by Josh Billings, our pint of beans (dried) are first soaked in water overnight, brought to the boil, and allowed to simmer for about 30 to 45 minutes. The least amount of boiling the harder the bean and the more nutty the flavour. There are many ways of serving and preparing them, given in detail in the chapter on recipes. So, in spite of the incredibility of the statement of Billings, our pint of dried soya beans is without doubt one of the most economic foods available.

It may be said that it is the cheapest food on the market, if you can obtain it, and yet the most health giving. It is hoped that this book will introduce strangers to the bean, stimulate their interest in this fine vegetable, and tempt them to try it. Others, who are conversant with the bean, and eat it in one or more of its numerous forms, as part of their diet, may learn more of its versatility, wonderful health giving properties, and realize what a wise choice they have made.

Wonder Food – God's Gift to Man

From time immemorial man has searched the wide world for everlasting youth and a perfect food. He, even in this atomic age, is almost as far away from success as ever in both these probes, except for the fact that he has the finest, if not the most perfect food, on his doorstep, if the Far East and places like the United States can be considered as being so close in the Jet Age.

Credit for this food goes to the ancient people of the Orient, who were the first to cultivate and proclaim the vital life giving secrets of the soya bean. Without exception it is, as yet, the most perfect food known to man, ever grown, and most unlikely to be excelled in the future. Our soya bean, although very small in size, is in protein, vitamin and mineral content undoubtedly the king of all beans. When it was first introduced into America it became known as the Japan Pea. For, dried in its natural shape, it is not a bit like a bean but is perfectly round, even smaller than a pea. Of a light yellow colour it has a tiny black dot upon it. After being soaked for 12 hours in water, the size is more than doubled and it takes on the shape of an ordinary dwarf bean.

For over 5,000 years this tiny seed has been the staple food of certain parts of the East, including North China, Japan, Korea and some areas of India. The ancient Yogis, who were among the world's first vegetarians, placed great faith in the soya bean as a supplement to their meatless diet.

If you read on, it is hoped that this short account of

the bean will show you that it not only earned such a high place in the minds of the ancient peoples of the Far East and India but even today in our twentieth century the tiny little bean is still to be revered.

Many Valuable Foods and Essentials in One Plant

The soya bean is a wonderful source of vital goodness. Nutritionally, there is no other food that compares with it. It is the only vegetable which gives complete protein which compares with, and is in fact identical to, all forms of animal meats. It is really as good as eggs, milk and any other protein food. In fact superior in many ways (The writer is not a vegetarian, but only a moderate meat eater). The protein content alone of the bean is enormously high, being over 35%. It has 18% fat and is very rich in vitamins, trace elements, copper, iron and other ingredients vital for the development of healthy bones and bodies.

This is not the end of our story of this beanfeast, for its crowning glory lies in the fact that it is rich in lecithin, plant sterols and unsaturated fatty acids. Lecithin plays a most important part in lowering the amount of cholesterol in the blood stream, thereby helping to prevent coronary heart disease and weaknesses of the arteries. Fuller details of the bean's vitamin, mineral and other qualities are given in a later chapter.

Increase in Popularity of Soya Beans

A great change is taking place in the eating habits of many countries today. As forecast when this book was first written almost ten years ago, many parts of the world are having to cope with an increase in population and a shortage of protein from animal sources. So a renewed interest is being taken in many vegetable proteins of which the soya bean and soya protein foods hold pride of place. These foods are economical by comparison to meat and easy to obtain.

CHAPTER TWO

HISTORY OF THE SOYA BEAN

As stated, the little bean was shown to have been first cultivated in the Far East long before recorded history. Records have been traced in China giving details of planting of crops over 2,000 years before Christ. Advice to growers in those ancient times on soil conditions, types of crops and cultivation hints were found all in great detail. Just like the present day farmers guide to the planting and rotation of grain crops and so on. All this was taking place in times when the modern methods of agriculture were beyond anyone's wildest dreams.

Cultivation and Importance to the East

Grown as an annual crop it is without doubt the most important legume cultivated in Japan, Korea, North China and parts of India. Many Indian castes are vegetarians and the cow is considered a sacred animal and not allowed to be slaughtered under any circumstances. Perhaps this is why the Almighty allowed a bean equally as nourishing to flourish in this part of the world. For this and other reasons, to many of the varied and differing races of the East, the soya bean is not simply taken for granted as a vegetable but has earned the title 'the meat of the soil'.

Those ancient races of China and Japan were so impressed and thankful for their crops of soya beans that it was held in very high esteem, and in fact was classed as being one of the 'Five Sacred Grains'. Such crops were not only considered sacred and being in every way vital to the health, but essential to the existence of these ancient civilizations. So it will be appreciated what regard these people had for the soya bean then, and still have today, 5,000 years later. It has withstood the test of time from one generation to another and plays just as much a vital role now as it did then. The four other cultivations which made up the five sacred grains were those of barley, rice, wheat and millet.

Many useful inventions, customs and traditions have been passed down from the wise Chinese and other Eastern Races. Without doubt, although little realized, the greatest contribution they have made to the world in regard to food, is the production and continuous cultivation of the fabulous little soya bean. They were always aware of the fact that the bean is almost 'a miracle food'. Unfortunately, people in many other countries, even if they know of the existence of this crop are not prepared to accept something which is predominantly Eastern in origin. Little do they realize what they are missing in food value, but I hope this booklet may enlighten some of them.

Other Areas of Cultivation

Attempts to cultivate the bean in Europe have not met with great success. It is a loss to the people of these countries that this crop will only really do well in warmer climates. However, in more recent years it has been grown with some success in Russia, and the Americans have made tremendous advances, being today one of the largest producers of soya beans in the world. Between the two wars a flourishing industry revolving round the soya bean has sprung up in the U.S.A. Attempts have also been made with varying results to cultivate the bean in Australia, New Zealand, Manchuria, The Philippines, Formosa and Thailand.

Success has also been achieved by crops cultivated in Sweden, South Africa, Brazil, New Zealand, Pakistan, USSR, Indonesia, Guatemala, India, Kenya, Korea and Canada.

Soya Beans in Europe

Credit for bringing the news of the soya bean to Europe goes to a German botanist Englebert Kaempfer. Towards the latter part of the seventeenth century he spent some three years in Japan and described the bean as being similar to a lupin with seeds of a pea. Interest in the crop did not materialize in Europe for nearly another 100 years. In 1875, successful crops of different varieties of the bean were cultivated in Austria by Fredrich Haberlandt. The result was that four good strains appeared in Austria, Hungary and other countries and reasonable crops were grown.

Haberlandt's efforts did much to promote interest in the growing of the bean. In 1739, packets of the seed were taken to France by Missionaries from China, but it was not cultivated for another 40 years, when some Chinese soya beans were grown in the Marseilles area. Likewise, Italians were able to plant the bean in about 1840 but it was never cultivated as a major crop. This is unfortunate, the Italians, undoubtedly have the ideal warm climate in which it would flourish. An attempt, with limited success was made to grow it at Kew Gardens, England. The English climate is far too cold for the crop to do well.

Ignorance of the True Value of the Bean

During these early days of crop cultivation in Europe, and unfortunately even today, people considered the bean to be unfit for human consumption. No doubt many thought it to be an ideal food for Chinese coolies, or Rickshaw boys. What a feast it was for them – how they could run with a rickshaw all day long, or work like beavers refuelling a ship with heavy baskets of coal with no ill effects.

Others, farmers included, felt that the bean was ideal as cattle fodder and equally as good if sown, allowed to grow and then ploughed back into the soil as a green manure. This is, of course, really rather tragic, but it must be remembered, only in America and Europe in comparatively recent years, scientists and doctors alike have come to realize the necessity of vitamins to health, together with a reasonable amount of minerals and protein.

Furthermore, it is only during the last few years of investigation into stress, heart diseases and other illnesses of modern society, that the real value of the soya bean has been revealed. In 30 years' personal experience of the soya bean as a food – I have found it to be second to none.

History of the Soya Bean – U.S.A.

In his writings in 1840, a certain James Mease reported the bean to be flourishing in the Pennsylvania area of America. Later, in 1854, some varieties were brought to the U.S.A. from Japan – and at that time it very appropriately became known as the Japan pea. For many years which followed the bean was simply used by farmers in America as food for livestock, or ploughed into the fields as manure.

The Perry expedition to Japan brought back strains of the bean to the U.S.A. in approximately 1854, with the ideal climatic conditions prevailing the crops were very good. It was in 1882 that the Carolina Experimental Agriculture Station grew what became known

HISTORY OF THE SOYA BEAN

as the Mammoth Yellow Soya Bean, which proved an excellent cropper and ideal for growing.

In 1889 a representative of the Massachusetts Agriculture Experimental Station introduced a large number of species of the bean into the States. The Kansas Agricultural Experimental Station likewise carried out tests and experiments on large scale growing of the crop. Realizing the possibilities for American farmers, the U.S. Department of Agriculture introduced large numbers, in fact over 10,000 species of soya beans, mostly from Asia, with a few varieties from Europe.

By 1936 the Americans were well on the way to becoming the world's largest growers of the soya bean. The U.S.A. and the Canadian Departments of Agriculture co-operated to produce better and improved varieties of seed. Vast amounts of work and experiments conducted resulted in bigger and better crops of beans, with correspondingly greater yields of soya bean oil. The value of the crops increased annually and a new industry was formed.

Major American Industry

During the past 60 years the Americans have become the world's largest growers of the soya bean. It is indeed remarkable, in fact almost unbelievable, to what uses, both as a food and a drink, and for industrial purposes the soya bean has been put to in the U.S.A. This does not include uses on the farm as manure and fodder for animals.

A further book could well be written on the commercial aspects of the bean in the States. However, as we are looking at it from the food value, a brief account of its other very numerous uses will be given in a later chapter. To me it seems a criminal waste of a perfect food to use soya beans to further man's end in the manufacturing world, especially at a time when millions are on the verge of, if not exactly, starving.

The Fiskeby V – Temperate Climate Soya Bean

Until the Second World War attempts to cultivate crops of soya beans in many parts of the world met with limited success and sometimes proved disastrous. However, an amazing exception to this was in Sweden, where, for many decades excellent crops have been harvested from a completely new strain of bean. This crop has become known as The Fiskeby V Soya Bean (Fiskeby being the name of the village where it was first grown).

This new species of soya bean was perhaps very much over rated when described as being, 'The most important new food in the history of the planet.' Unfortunately, to date it has not lived up to this mighty claim, for results achieved by many gardeners and associations have failed to justify these praises. In fairness it must be recorded that adverse weather conditions which prevailed in England during many of the years when these crops were cultured may well have been a deciding factor in reducing the chances of success of many growers.

Another interesting feature in soya bean cultivation concerns the necessity of growing crops on the same soil year after year. Soya beans in common with some other crops are known to progessively build up their own nutrients in the soil. Whilst this is taking place the first few years harvests are generally expected to be far below the crop's full potential.

CHAPTER THREE

CONTENT OF SOYA BEANS

With an abundance of vital bodily needs, soya beans contain over 40% protein and about 20% fat, or bean oil. This vegetable oil is ideal as it does not cause any great increase in consumers' body weight, like animal fats.

Proteins are made up of amino acids, of which there are 22 in all. The soya bean is one of the few foods that contain all 22 of the health giving amino acids. As such it is considered a complete protein food. These beans are very rich in lecithin, a wonderful protector of the heart and arteries (amino acids and lecithin are discussed in greater detail in Chapter IV).

Soya bean sprouts, or bean shoots, as they are sometimes called, contain vitamin A and are rich in vitamin C. Likewise, the bean is a good source of vitamins B and E. Minerals and trace elements are also present, these include copper, iron, calcium, magnesium, zinc, manganese, nitrogen, phosphorus, potassium and sulphur.

The rich supply of protein, vitamins and minerals build strong healthy bones and help protect the body from disease and sickness. All these ingredients of the bean play a fundamental part, as we shall see, in the efficient functioning of our bodies.

Protein

What is it? The word means primary, or first place and this is what it is to human beings and animals. We are made up of protein and every part of our body contains it. Body cells make up tissues, and each and every one of the millions of cells relies on a supply of protein to counteract daily wear and tear, and maintain good health. The body is able and can store a limited amount of protein, but this is quickly used up if daily supplies cease, or are reduced to a low level. The main function of protein is body repair and to generate heat and energy.

Naturally, persons who are overweight need to control their daily intake of protein. Others who are thin can beneficially add protein to their diet. As is the case with all foods and vitamins, to consume excessive amounts may well do more harm than good. Moderation in all things is the way to healthy existence, and eating is no exception to this rule.

Amino Acids
It was not realized for a long time that various proteins are made up of nitrogen, and up to 22 amino acids. Most body cells require all these for perfect development and functioning. When protein is consumed it is broken down by the body into the various amino acids which are carried by the blood stream to every cell, this process being continued as long as we live.

Wonderful Functioning of the Body
A remarkable thing is that the cells of the body are able to produce 14 of the 22 amino acids. Protein, fat, sugar and nitrogen are used for this purpose. However, there are 8 amino acids which the body cannot manufacture, which are sometimes referred to as being 'the essential amino acids'. In order to enjoy good health it is vital that these are present in our daily diet. From this it will be appreciated how important it is to have not only sufficient protein, but a reasonable amount which contains all the 22 amino acids.

Foods Rich in Protein

Many foods contain a good supply of protein including: meats, liver, milk and all milk products, yeast, millet, sunflower seeds, cereals, nuts and other seeds, including the richest source of vegetable protein, the soya bean and its products. Foods with all the 22 amino acids, that is, complete protein, are meats, eggs, liver, milk, brewer's yeast, wheat germ, nuts and soya beans. It is interesting to note that the amino acid analysis of soya beans and casein (composition of meat) are almost identical in every way. The only food other than meat which has anything like the protein content of soya products is skimmed, dried milk. Half a cup of skimmed milk is as nutritious as a quart of fresh milk. The reason for this is quite simple for all the essential ingredients of the milk powder are present in the skimmed part and not contained in either the cream or water.

Lack of Protein

In spite of being able to store some protein, if the body does not receive an adequate daily supply, eventually ageing will surely occur. If this state of affairs continues with modern stress, muscles will eventually begin to lose tone and degeneration of the body will set in. All manner of illnesses can be attributed to lack of sufficient protein over the years. Poor circulation, chilblains, constipation.

A rather dangerous situation can develop because protein deficiency over a long period can be concealed by eating large amounts of devitalized foodstuffs, such as sugars, processed refined foods, white flours and starchy preparations. But the time will come when the body can no longer continue to function properly without the recuperative intake of protein, and lack of it will result in illness and disease.

The supply of protein in the body can easily be depleted by persons who worry and suffer anxiety. Those to whom the stresses and strains of daily living are too great, need far more protein than the characters who are carefree, unruffled, and can take life in their stride. Even today a surprising number of diets are sadly lacking in sufficient protein. So in order to remain healthy, young and full of vitality it is essential to obtain enough protein daily. Every part of you is made up of protein, and there is no easier, cheaper or tastier way of getting it than by consuming the soya bean and its products.

Lecithin

If the vigour and vitality that made you feel that it was good simply to be alive has gone, it may well be your body lacks lecithin. This is an ingredient of soya beans and wheat germ which plays a vital part in building up nervous energy in your body. It contains other substances which help prevent fatty deposits being formed in the arteries and other places. The bean has so many things that are good for us but lecithin is that little something extra which places it on its own as a king above all beans. A more detailed account of the way in which lecithin helps prevent ageing and restores lost youth follows in the next chapter.

Vitamin A

An adequate supply of this vitamin counteracts infectious diseases. Shortage will cause all manner of complaints affecting the breathing system, bronchial tubes, and even the lungs. It can very soon cause defective eyesight if persons are deprived of it for a long period.

Vitamin C. (Ascorbic Acid)
Bean sprouts are very rich in this essential vitamin. Acute shortage of it will lead to scurvy, as experienced by sailors before faster steamships were built. It is essential to obtain a regular supply of vitamin C because the body is unable to store it. Signs that a person is not getting a sufficient intake are tiredness, despair, poor healing flesh, and bleeding gums.

Vitamin B.
Today far more is being learnt about the food content of the B vitamin group. It has now been established that, including vitamin B12, there are no less than 11 vitamins in this group. Five of the eleven are present in soya beans, namely, thiamine, riboflavin, niacin, choline and inositol. Of all these 11 vitamins, three are considered most important for the body – the bean contains these three, being the first three mentioned – thiamine, riboflavin and niacin.

We will very briefly examine these three and see what they will do for us.

Thiamine
Sometimes called aneurine. Shortage results in stunted growth and depression. If it is withheld for a long period, beri-beri might occur. It feeds the nerves, aids appetite, and can prevent a large number of minor disorders, such as constipation and other complaints, which, if neglected for years, will cause serious illness.

Riboflavin(B2.)
This ingredient of the bean protects the muscles of the eyes, the skin, hair and finger nails. Shortage will result in cracked lips and corners of the mouth. The tongue may become sore and a burning sensation is caused. Women are more prone to a shortage of riboflavin.

Niacin (Nicotinic Acid)
This is sometimes known as the antipellagra vitamin. A serious deficiency of niacin will produce mental problems. Signs of a shortage are: rough skin, sore tongue and diarrhoea. The entire mucous membranes of the mouth, nose and throat are affected.

Vitamin E
This is sometimes known as the fertility vitamin. In recent times vitamin E has proved effective in healing various heart complaints. Such illnesses as thrombosis, phlebitis and ulcers have responded well to vitamin E treatment. It has also been used successfully to cope with menopause problems, to improve muscle tone and overcome poor circulation.

Copper
A component of the bean, and another mineral seldom considered by the average person to have any effect on our bodies. People are aware that iron is vital for a rich blood stream, and calcium essential for strong teeth and bones, but know nothing about copper. It aids the body's digestive processes and carries out vital work, though not in such a spectacular way, of helping convert iron into hemoglobin (the oxygen supplying substance in red blood cells). This process is vital for the prevention of anaemia. Lack of sufficient copper in the body may well cause faulty respiration and general bodily weakness.

Iron
Undoubtedly one of the most important minerals needed by man. It controls the body's built-in thermostat, ensuring that we are warm in cold weather. More important, it gives vitality, strength, endurance, and

staying power. In fact it helps us to obtain from life all these things which are worthwhile, lack of which brings misery and unhappiness. So iron is another vital contribution of the bean.

Calcium

Is really a wonderful element of the soya bean. Vital in man for the development of strong healthy bones and teeth. Experiments among animals given calcium shows that they live longer, and retain sexual powers well into old age. Whether humans receive the same benefits remains to be proved.

Fat Content

About one fifth of the bean is composed of fat or if reduced, to soya oil. It is of interest that this fat, or oil, is immediately assimilated by the body during daily activity, during the course of repair to vital organs, nerves and cells. So fortunately we do not store the rather high fat content of this vegetable, as we would animal fat. Thus, with its massive supply of protein and fat that will not induce obesity the bean is equally good and nutritious for the under and over-weight consumer.

Vegetarians and the Soya Bean

Whether or not you decide to become a vegetarian, is indeed a personal choice. It may depend on religious convictions, conscience and so on. However, much depends on climatic conditions. One can hardly expect an Eskimo to adopt a vegetarian diet, living in a barren waste, with temperatures well below freezing all the year round. The intense cold of the Arctic and other places make increasing demands upon the constitution, which many feel can only be satisfied on a diet rich in meat.

In semi-tropical places and on the equator, the demand for meat dishes is considerably less. Vegetarian foodstuffs are much more satisfying in a hot climate, so it is fitting that the soya bean flourishes under these conditions, where it is in greatest demand. Unlike meat eaters, it is a far greater problem for vegetarians to ensure they get an adequate daily intake of protein. A regular supply of vegetables and drinks rich in protein is important.

The most well-known protein foods have been mentioned, but for the benefit of vegetarians, the three essential foods are soya beans and the product of the bean, skimmed milk powder and nuts, in particular brazil nuts. Throughout the ages the bean has fully earned its description as 'the meat of the soil' and as such it is God's gift to everyone, but in particular to those following a meatless diet. In fact, by replacing meat with soya beans, and bean products, vegetarians are getting their protein direct from the soil, whereas meat eaters are really making use of second class protein.

Vegans
For followers of the Vegan diet, which excludes both meat and eggs, I would suggest that the soya bean and as many of its products as can be obtained is a *must* and should be eaten daily without fail.

Future for the Hungry People of the World
Milk was always accepted as being the most perfect food for human beings. However, in soya beans we have a variety of nourishment which excels anything ever produced in the past. America is still the largest grower of soya beans in the world and has in recent years exported 50% or more of her products. To try to give some indication of the magnitude of the United States

soya bean crop the 1979 output had a total cash value of £34 million. Undoubtedly, such a supply of health giving food, which can be utilized in many different forms, should prove a Godsend to prevent starvation among the millions living in underdeveloped countries.

CHAPTER FOUR

ABOUT LECITHIN – VITAL FOR RETAINING YOUTH

In many countries today people have every prospect of living longer, and of being able to remain active well into old age. Your date of birth is not now the only, or most deciding factor of when you are old. There are renowned examples of men and women who have defied the calendar. Winston Churchill became Prime Minister at 65. Conrad Adenauer, leader of post-war Germany, known to the people as 'Der Alte', was leading a great nation at the age of 85. Such brave exploits of men like Chichester and Alec Rose, who at 65 years of age sailed round the world single-handed.

In Western civilization the population of countries becomes an older one, there are more people than ever before living to retirement age and a remarkable number who now complete their century. Not many years ago it was unusual to meet a person of 100 years of age – not so today. However, in spite of this extensive increase in life span, many unfortunate people do age quickly, for example deaths from heart disease and cancer have never been so high.

Certain factors do contribute towards life expectancy – those whose parents and grandparents lived to a ripe old age can reasonably expect to do likewise. However, in spite of setbacks such as these which are beyond our control, we are to a far greater extent than many realize, masters of our own destiny. 'We are today, what we were yesterday, and we will be tomorrow, what we are today.' Time does not stand still.

Our bodies can only be made up of what we put into

them in the form of food and drink. Thus, to spend years consuming devitalized processed foods can eventually produce a human body, tired and weary, as equally deprived of vitality as the unwholesome diet received. To be healthy, and remain in good physical condition, it is imperative to eat wholesome, natural food as God provided it. Plenty of fresh fruits and vegetables, whole meal flour products, little or no refined sugars. Such sweeteners as honey, fruit juices and natural brown sugars are by far the best.

Many pay far more attention to the running of a car engine, or lawn mower, than to their own bodies. Inferior oils and misuse will soon ruin an engine. Fortunately, devitalized feeding, even over a long period will not permanently turn anyone into a weakling or chronic invalid. The human body, even after gross neglect, has a wonderful way of responding to correct food and healthy living. In recent times, scientists, doctors and others have shown that approximately every seven years for a long period of our lives practically every part of the human body has been replaced. So it is never too late to mend. An almost miraculous change can be brought about by getting nourishing food and other essentials that make life worth living.

What is Lecithin?

It is a food substance, rich in choline and inositol, which is derived from certain foods, such as egg yolk, wheat germ, and by far the richest source – soya beans. Apart from an abundance of protein, and all the other goodness, lecithin is that little extra ingredient which makes the soya bean superior to any kind of food known to man. When those ancient people christened the bean 'the meat of the soil', they were thinking only in terms of a satisfying food which would more than replace vital protein elements of a meat diet. Little did they dream about lecithin, for it was a long time indeed before the evidence of the presence of this substance in the crops was revealed.

Lecithin is utilized by the human body to build up much of the tissues of nerves and brain. About one third of our brains and a fifth of our nerves are composed of it. In our nervous system it is used to produce electricity. Lack of this substance in our diet will eventually lead to nervous exhaustion, for it is actually an ingredient of nerve tissues. For many, who lack enthusiasm for living, lecithin might well prove to be the difference to them of being alive – or just existing. So, in simple terms lecithin is really a substance which contains generating power for the smooth running of the body, just as an effective dynamo will keep an engine running.

Cholesterol

This is a fatty kind of residue that builds up in the bloodstream and causes arteries to become furred up. It is believed to be contained in animal fats, but even experts have differing opinions of cause of cholestrol. It is very interesting to note, however, that strokes and heart diseases increase directly in proportion to a country's industrial development.

Western civilization has a high rate of death from strokes. The populations of these areas are able to, and do consume a plentiful supply of calories, dairy produce, fat, together with a high intake of refined sugar, white flour and all manner of processed foods. Where people are living on more natural foods there is a far less incidence of strokes. Vegetarians show lower incidence of strokes than usual.

Generally, the greater the physical activity, the less chance there is of getting heart disease and strokes.

This is clearly shown in U.S.A. and England – where professional and clerical workers have the greatest risk and agricultural and manual workers the lowest.

Choline
This component of lecithin aids in the prevention of fatty deposits in the body, not only about the midsection, which is the most likely place for it to form, but in vital parts of the arteries, heart and liver. Choline, by emulsifying such fatty deposits, enables the body to dispose of them. Just as a really fine motor oil will keep an engine running clean for a long time, choline will do likewise for the human body.

Inositol
The other vital substance of lecithin nourishes the heart and provides it with regular power. It will also aid the disposal of fatty substances which have been building up in the arteries.

It is only in more recent times, that scientists and other experts, have become aware of the vital role, played by lecithin in protecting health. Lecithin in tablet form may be purchased from all health food stores. So a person who is unable to obtain or does not like such food as soya beans or wheat germ, is able to get this vital ingredient in tablet form. In this respect, it is always advisable, to insist on obtaining a supply in its natural organic form, not a synthetic product, but something pure and straight from the plant, as nature intended.

The Elderly
The amazing results of the dispersal of fats in the blood of the elderly, by the use of lecithin is even more pronounced. There is a tendency for fats to remain in the

blood of older persons longer. Edward F. Hewitt writes in his book, *The Years Between 75 & 90*, 'If lecithin is given to older people before a fatty meal it has been found that the fats in the blood return to normal in a short time, in the same way as they do in younger persons'. Having heard a brief introduction into the wonders of lecithin – it is hardly surprising that the soya bean made its mark in ancient history, and is considered such a vital food today.

CHAPTER FIVE

THE SOYA BEAN IN THE FAR EAST

For centuries the Chinese have considered the art of cookery as playing a vital role in their lives, equal in every way to all the other arts in their society. Generally speaking, people in Europe know very little about the Chinese, their way of life, and in particular Eastern Food, although the opening of thousands of Chinese restaurants has made some amends for this. An old Chinese belief, which is just as true today as it was centuries ago, is that a man becomes what he eats. The record of survival in China during the last 5,000 years and the fact that they have the largest population in the world would indicate that they eat the right food.

In a vast continent, in fact larger than the whole of Europe, as may be imagined there are literally thousands of ways of cooking and preparing food. However, broadly speaking all Chinese dishes are classed under five headings – or Schools of Cookery. Canton is one such School and many of the better Chinese Restaurants in Europe and elsewhere are Cantonese. The reason is that Cantonese cookery can easily be adapted for international use, and the bulk of the Chinese living abroad are Cantonese. They have a great variety of sea foods, and are experts at preserving them by salting and then drying them in the sun. They have introduced a greater number of dishes than any other school.

As this book concerns soya beans we will look at the Chinese vegetable cooking. Basically all schools have the same ingredients. They all use soya, peanut or other vegetable oil, not animal fat. There is no doubt that the appetizing health-giving soya sauce plays a vital role in food preparation. They have many tasty and skilfully prepared vegetable dishes, including the soya bean and its products. Dishes are made to resemble the shape of fowl, fish, ham, etc., and then covered with soya bean curd skin. (This consists of bean curd, as thin as paper, seasoned with soya sauce and dried.)

Chinese vegetable soup will resemble chicken broth in every way. Really it is soup made from soya bean sprouts. What a fine thing for vegetarians, who have meat eaters as friends, to be able to serve up a meal for them which looks like meat, tastes like it, but is really vegetable so prepared and tasty, that even an expert would find it difficult to distinguish any difference.

Soya Sauce

Known to the Chinese as Soy sauce, it is one of the outstanding culinary inventions of the Chinese and is extensively used, as a condiment, or to replace salt at the table. So the Chinese automatically get a certain amount of this ancient food every time they sit down to a meal. This sauce enhances the taste of all food, but to obtain the right fragrance it should be used sparingly, otherwise the taste of the sauce will dominate the entire meal. Customers of Chinese restaurants will be familiar with the bottles of this sauce placed on each table.

Bean Curd or Tofu

A food used extensively throughout China – a National dish to be found in palaces, or among the peasants. It is obtained by bringing soya bean milk to the boil, when a film forms on the surface, this is known as yuba. Yuba is a very valuable health giving food extremely rich in protein. In preparation for eating, it can be either dried, or used in soups, gravies or with other dishes. Bean curd is without a doubt a masterpiece of the Chinese in food preparation. Although one of the cheapest foods obtainable anywhere in the world – it can easily be produced as a delicacy at a banquet fit for a king. Bean curd is so universally accepted that every Chinese School of cookery has its own special way of preparing it.

Bean Sprouts

Sometimes referred to as shoots! Two kinds are used in China, those of the soya and mung beans. The latter known as green peas. These two vegetables are unique, because of the fact that they can be grown anywhere in a few days, throughout the year, given the necessary time and attention of which the Chinese have both at their disposal. These shoots are delicious and very rich in vitamin C – served with meals in Chinese restaurants as Chow Mein or Chop Suey. These sprouts are eaten by the Chinese as a green vegetable and served as a salad.

Soya Bean Milk

Records show that this was used long before the birth of Christ. This may be consumed fresh, in the same manner as we use cow's milk. A vegetable cheese can be prepared from this milk, in much the same way as the farmer obtains cheese from cows' milk. This is very similar to bean curd or tofu previously described.

Candied Beans

This is when the beans are boiled as a sweet in syrup. They can also be soaked in water and then roasted – very similar to roasted nuts.

There are many other and varied ways in which the

Chinese make use of the bean but this brief account shows the main ones.

Japan
Many of the uses of the soya bean in China apply equally to Japan. However, the Japanese crop is only a fraction of that grown in China.

Natto and Miso
These two foods are famous in Japan and used everywhere. Both are obtained from the soya bean by a process of fermenting and steaming. A variety called Red Miso is produced by using soya beans, together with a large quantity of salt, and after preparation it will keep for many years.

Japanese Soya Sauce
Is obtained by fermenting beans with parched wheat.

CHAPTER SIX

AMERICAN INFLUENCE ON THE SOYA BEAN

Although the history of the soya bean goes back over 5,000 years in the Far East, it is only a fairly recent crop in America. The last few decades have seen a phenomenal increase in acreage of these beans in the United States. It took the Americans a long time to realize the crop had tremendous possibilities, not only as food for the home market, but as an export crop. Later, scientists proved that it was very useful, and equally versatile for industrial uses. Gradually, they began to appreciate why the crop had been classed as a 'sacred grain' by the ancient Chinese. Cultivation progressed rapidly and China slowly lost her lead as the world's largest producer to the Americans.

By 1960, China with the largest population in the world, was growing only about half the soya bean acreage of the United States. A further disadvantage from the export point of view, for the Chinese with 700,000,000 mouths to feed, was that the bulk of their crop was no doubt earmarked for the home market. So the Americans had two distinct advantages over China:

1. On being able to cultivate twice their acreage of soya beans.
2. Being the leading industrial power in the world, and with a much smaller population, they were able to utilize much of their crop for export purposes. What a wonderful job they have done in putting the soya bean on the map for Western civilization.

Culture and Development of the Soya Bean in the U.S.A.

These beans have been grown in the United States for well over 100 years. Tonnage of two crops for 1920 and 1979 will illustrate how cultivation has progressed bringing America into the world lead:

In 1920 there were only 190,000 acres under cultivation. By 1979 this had increased to the enormous crop estimated at 28.5 million hectares. Soya oil ranked as the largest among all the oil seed crops of the Western Hemisphere. The bean became fourth in the cash crops of America. This must be, without exception, a record expansion of any crop throughout the world. This is really remarkable, when we consider that prior to 1940, in the States, the bean had only been grown for hay, or used as a green manure. The crop showed that it had many unusual features. Not only was it very rich in both protein, oil and other essential vitamins, minerals, as outlined in a previous chapter, but it would thrive on indifferent soils. Another great advantage of the crop was that it had the attraction of being almost immune from disease.

Diseases of Crops

Effects of diseases on soya beans have been considered in the past to have been of little importance, and until recently there was little information on disease damage to crops. It is of interest, that most of the diseases of the soya bean do not kill it, but simply reduce its ability to crop. Some 12 diseases are known but, as stated, they seldom cause termination of growth.

Insects and Spider Mites

The crops may be attacked by a variety of pests but usually they do survive. However, occasionally certain insects such as caterpillars have been known to devastate an entire crop. Certain approved chemical fertilisers are used to control such beetles and caterpillars that may cause damage.

Disease Resistant Varieties
Much progress has been made in recent years in the U.S.A., where they have produced new strains of soya bean crops. These are disease-resistant and heavy croppers.

Influence on American Food
The intensive growth of this crop in the United States brought with it many changes in eating habits. The bean and substitutes of it, were incorporated into a wide range of foods, especially when people began to realize how healthy soya foods really are.

Meat and Vegetables in One Crop
The soya bean, christened 'The Meat of the Soil' 5,000 years ago by those wise old Chinese farmers, has been proved as such in the twentieth century by American scientists. Many organizations in America have been experimenting in the manufacture of ersatz foods. The astounding results are: Chicken, turkey, pork, duck, ham and so on – you name the meat dish, they produce it – as simple as that. These reproductions of our Sunday roast or Christmas turkey are mainly constituted of soya bean proteins.

There are an estimated fifty million or more Americans, who, for one reason or another prefer a meatless diet. The future looks very rosy for them. They can now get tasty, meaty, soya foods as a replacement – and the remarkable thing is that from the taste they will not realize they have changed to vegetarian food.

Milk and Milk Substitutes

Not content with meat and vegetables growing on the beanstalk, Americans are now able to obtain a wide range of soya milk products. These include ordinary milk, cream, cake fillings and ice cream. However, as yet soya milk does not taste exactly like fresh cow's milk. It rather resembles reconstituted milk. It will be impossible to completely disguise the difference in taste between plant milk and cow's milk, though nutritiously it remains supreme.

Other Products

The American housewife, in addition to these rather astounding foods from the bean has:

Soya flour: This can be used for the making of tasty health giving bread or cakes. Also to add protein and goodness to ordinary flours, soups and gravies.

Bean sprouts: Similar in every way to those produced by the Chinese and Japanese, and outlined in a previous chapter. The Americans have an extensive canning and freezing industry to deal with much of their bean produce.

Soya flour, grits, flakes used by the Americans for cake, bread and famous doughnut making. They also utilize bean products for the purpose of making noodles, breakfast cereals, macaroni and various health foods. The bean is roasted like a nut, and used as a sweet after being cooked in syrup. A high percentage of the oil of the American soya crop is used for margarine, salad and cooking oils.

American Soya Bean Association

Founded in 1920 to protect the interest of soya bean

producers and handlers. A most efficient organization bringing together all connected with the industry in any way. The main objects of the Association : to safeguard the future of the crop and promote markets, a monthly magazine *The Soya Bean Digest* and an *Annual Blue Book of Soya Beans* are published.

The headquarters of The American Soya Bean Association is at Hudson, Iowa, U.S.A. A hive of activity exists at the executive office where many thousands of queries are answered annually about every aspect of the soya bean crop.

Educational Films

A number of coloured films are used for training and educational purposes showing the cultivation of the soya bean at every stage. The association has these films for the use of growers, distributors, soya protein food industries, and all others interested in any way in the soya bean, including school children.

Japan

In 1956 The American Soya Bean Association made an agreement with Japan to establish a Soya Bean Market Development Project. This came into being with the formation of the Japanese American Soya Bean Institute in Tokyo. The institute has done a great deal to promote all aspects of the vast soya bean industry. Japanese trade groups have visited the U.S.A to see for themselves how the industry works. Trade Fairs in Japan have been sponsored where U.S. soya beans and all the bean products have been exhibited. There has been a tremendous increase in the consumption of soya oil and other products in Japan since the institute was formed. Also the protein content of the crops have been used more by the Japanse in group feedings in factories and offices.

Soya Proteins in Foods

Forgive repetition if I again quote that, 'only a minor part of the protein of the American soya crop is used in human foods' at present. The consolation is that this percentage is steadily increasing. This has been brought about by the remarkable way soya protein can simulate all meat dishes. This is indeed exciting news for the average American, most of whom are as ignorant of the soya protein meats industries as the man in the street in England.

For many years now in the U.S.A. soya proteins have been extensively used as a low per cent additive to a wide range of foods including: biscuits, cereals, muffins, bread rolls, cakes, frankfurters, sausages, meat patties, meat loaves, gravy, poultry, soups, puddings, candy, confection, baby foods and other items. These proteins are used in a greater percentage in health foods.

Advantages of Soya Proteins

These protein additives have many great attractions. They are very nutritious, containing all the amino acids vital for good health. Being moisture retainers, emulsifiers and binders, they have many other uses. Shelf life of such products is greatly increased. Appearance of food is improved and processing costs reduced. Finally soya flour, grits and meal contain a rich supply of B complex vitamins, choline, calcium, iron, phosphorus, potassium and traces of other essential minerals.

Types of Soya Proteins

Some soya proteins are as old as the bean crop, being a food of ancient China centuries ago. These include soya milk, flour, and grits, others are as new as the Atomic Age. It is interesting to note that isolated soya protein prepared from defatted soya flakes is almost pure protein, being 90-98% on a moisture free basis. It has a fine flavour, pleasant aroma and consists of a fine creamy white powder. These concentrates were introduced in 1960 and show, beyond doubt, that from a nutritional point of view the soya bean can do more than hold its own with animal protein.

Finally, a look at what the writer considers the greatest achievement by American soya processors, the textured and spun proteins. These cover the very wide range of new simulated meats, resembling such foods as turkey, chicken, bacon, beef, and sausage. In fact, you name the meat or fowl, and the soya protein foods provide it. With these foods it must be remembered that you are getting whole goodness, with no shrinkage, bone, skin or excess fat. Joints of meat shrink considerably on roasting, not soya meats. Also the food needs virtually no cooking. What a boon to one's wife to have a Sunday joint or Christmas or Thanksgiving turkey that only requires warming up! The only thing missing is the 'wish bone' to pull over the Christmas dinner table and that, I am sure, can be introduced for the occasion.

Spun Proteins

These are produced by spinning the isolated soya protein into fibres which are combined with flavours, fats, and binders, to process them into simulated meats. An item of food similar in every way to meat. It can be obtained dried like cold meat or in a moist state resembling cooked meat.

Textured Proteins

Obtained by a special extrusion type-processing of soya flour, these provide a high protein food which can be prepared in almost any colour or flavour. Such protein keeps its shape and texture even when placed in water and has the appearance and taste of every range of meats.

For those who do not like the taste of meat this versatile protein can be produced to taste like other products such as nuts or sweets. Textured protein does not have the uniform fibrosity of meat and is produced in chunks or pieces of various sizes from small grits to pieces from one-half to three-quarters of an inch in diameter. The protein and fat content can be controlled and, like spun protein, there is no shrinkage or wastage in skin and bones. Textured proteins are much cheaper than spun fibres and compare more than favourably with meat prices.

CHAPTER SEVEN

INDUSTRIAL USES IN AMERICA

Some details of the food value and uses of the soya bean and its numerous products as an aid to health have been given. From this it will be seen that as a complete protein and protective food, the soya bean rates as second to none. We now take a look at the role, an ever increasing one, that it is playing in the world of commerce.

Man, as always, has not been slow to exploit this crop to serve his purposes in industry. In Western society today many people are far more inclined to take a greater interest in cars, home decorations, and bigger and better gadgets, than in good health and wholesome food. The versatile little bean has aided them.

Paint Manufacture
For many years soya bean oil has been used for making excellent paints. These include white paints, used for domestic purposes in kitchens, and all manner of coloured paints for use in industry. This includes the spray painting of cars, machinery and many other allied uses. Soya bean oil has also been utilized for making resin paints and varnishes.

Printing Industry
Here the oil finds its way into the processes for the manufacture of printing inks, adhesives, paper and glues. With an ever increasing demand for more papers, periodicals and books this use is likely to be increased.

Brewing
In the U.S.A. the bean is used in the brewing industry

to provide nutrients to aid and assist the growing of yeast. By this means the flavours of many beers have been enhanced. This particular use of the bean may well be considered to be equally as much towards food production as industrial.

Plywood Industry
The remarkable adhesive power of soya glue has made a tremendous impact on the manufacture of plywood in the U.S.A. In fact, up to 1963, the total tonnage of bean glue used exceeded that of any other adhesive in the industry.

Pharmaceuticals
Once again, here we find that the oil of the bean plays an increasing role in the production of soaps, cosmetics, and other aids to beauty in the chemist's shop.

Other Uses
These include productions of various oils. Making of sealing and caulking compounds; in the manufacture of linoleum and oilcloth, plastics and textile fibres. Another use is in the making of fire appliances, where, it has been found the oil acts as an emulsifying agent.

No doubt, at the time of writing this book, more and more ways of using the bean to serve man in the twentieth century are being discovered. If the commercial uses of this vegetable ever equal the food value, then it will become an industrial wonder of the world.

There is little doubt that the soya bean is destined to play an ever increasing role, both as a food and for industrial purposes. Research and experiments continue, in which more use than ever will be found for this versatile crop. Little did those ancient Chinese realize what part their humble little bean would play, in the commercial world of the Atomic Age.

CHAPTER EIGHT

THE SOYA BEAN AND WORLD FOOD SHORTAGE

The American nation has rendered a valuable service to the entire world in cultivating a gigantic soya bean crop. From an experimental stage during 1936, rapid progress was made and in just over ten years they had practically doubled this crop. If the same miraculous intensive cropping of this bean can be carried out in other countries, with a suitable climate, there is more than a gleam of hope for the world's hungry people.

During the ten years that have elapsed since the first edition of this book was published the American soya bean crop has expanded beyond all expectations and the 1979 harvest was an all time record.

It is perhaps only to be expected that the most wealthy nation in the world, with millions of acres of land, much of it in an ideal climate for bean cultivation, should do so well with these crops. What is perhaps not realized is that in the twenty-first century, millions of lives, hanging in the balance through food shortage, could well be saved by the export of American soya products.

Expanding World Population

In practically every country the birth rate is going up. In Western countries people mature earlier, marry younger, and live longer. There are more persons over the age of 65 than ever before, and this figure is bound to increase.

While disputes and differing opinions are held over the use of contraceptives and legal abortions, the population of the world continues to increase at a most alarming rate. At the same time, in many countries towns are growing and agricultural land is being swallowed up. It is considered that an ever increasing problem will be caused in trying to feed the masses of people.

Change in Eating Habits Necessary

Vegetarians are the people who are going to reap immediate benefit from the growing soya protein industries. Likewise, such races as Hindus, who have always abstained from eating meat on religious grounds.

However, it is not a simple matter to get people who have been meat eaters all their lives to make sudden changes to vegetable − meat protein − diets. Many would not be persuaded by the fact that the new kind of meal resembles the old in taste. If people are faced with a food shortage, or eating synthetic meat, then there is little doubt they would soon get used to the new fare.

So one of the greatest obstacles to overcome will be to sell the idea of meat, milk and vegetables all from one crop of beans. For centuries, man, in many parts of the world, has accepted meat and poultry as being the mainstay of his diet. It may equally be thousands of years before a real noticeable change takes place.

During recent years the soya bean and all its derivatives, especially soya protein foods, have become widely acceptable in many countries. There's hardly a supermarket or grocery shop where these cannot be seen on display. In America soya protein foods are now widely used and play a part in all school meals from coast to coast. Likewise, in the United Kingdom many Educational Authorities now use them in school meals.

Future Prospects

There is a great demand for soya bean oil. It has the largest distribution of any food oil in the Western hemisphere. Likewise, the potential exists for selling the protein, for human consumption from this vast crop. Once prejudice has been overcome, and protein meat prices are able to compare favourably with those of fresh meat, the future should be bright for these newly formed protein meat companies.

Booming Soya Milk Industry

Not long ago the suggestion of a milk supply from beans would have been ridiculed as a fairy story. Today, the story has come true for the Vita Soy company of America, who market millions of bottles of this milk throughout countries in the Far East.

Soy milk has two great attractions, it is cheaper than cow's milk in the countries where it is sold, and secondly it is very nutritious. Richer than cow's milk in iron, calcium and phosphorus. It also has the added attraction of being much easier to assimilate than ordinary creamy cow's milk in a warmer climate.

The success of the 'Soy Milk' Company indicates that the markets are available, and can be exploited to the full – for the benefit of everyone concerned.

Many Varieties

The Worthington Foods, Worthington, Ohio, U.S.A., have also gone into the Soya Milk business in a big way. They produce a milk powder called Soyamel, of which there are many kinds including, Soyamel Banana Beverage, Malt Soyamel, Fortified Soyamel and Regular Soyamel. The essential food elements in Soyamel include protein, fat, carbohydrate, calcium and phosphorus. One quart of reconstituted Soyamel (which dissolves instantly in water) and takes about 4 oz (100 g) of powder to make, provides the following nutritive values:

Vitamin A	5,000 U.S.P. units	Naicinamide	15mg
,, D	400 ,, ,,	Calcium	750 ,,
,, E	10 ,, ,,	Phosphorus	750 ,,
,, C	100 mg	Copper	1.5 ,,
,, B1	2 ,,	Manganese	2 ,,
,, B2	3 ,,	Zinc	5 ,,
,, B6	2 ,,	Iron	15 ,,
,, B12	2 micrograms	Iodine	100 micrograms

It will be noted that all of these essential bodily needs have been mentioned in Chapter 3, *Content of Soya Beans*. So it is interesting to find out that soya milk is equally as nutritive as the fabulous bean.

One quart of Worthington Fortified Soyamel is one of the most health-giving drinks in the world. This amount consumed daily provides all the vitamin and minerals essential to health for a normal adult, in addition to the protein content and essential amino acids. The outstanding quality of Soyamel is its flavour, being free of the characteristic bean taste sometimes present in soya beverages.

This milk looks good, tastes good and is good. Being very versatile it is equally suitable for cereals, vegetable soups, cooking, baking and all the other purposes for which cow's milk may be used.

Plamil or Plantmilk

Supplies of soya milk powder are not obtainable in England. However, one company is actually producing what is in effect soya protein milk, in a concentrated

WORLD FOOD SHORTAGE

liquid form. Water is simply added and it is ready for serving. Containing soya protein, this product has all the advantages of cow's milk and is a good source of lecithin, vitamins A, B, B12, D and calcium. It is a pure food drink being free from animal fats, artificial colouring and preservatives. So although it may be some time before powder soya milk is produced on a large scale in England, the liquid soya protein milk is becoming increasingly popular, and proves ideal for persons unable to take cow's milk, or others who have been advised to reduce their intake of animal fats.

Much may be said, for and against, the development of the soya bean protein industry. Man will insist in having, whenever possible, a freedom of choice. Thousands may never become resigned to the idea of living on a vegetarian diet, even if the protein is equal in all respects to animal flesh. On the other hand the majority of confirmed vegetarians would never change to a meat diet. However, with all the facts and figures, and arguments for and against, the introduction of 'meat of the soil', only man can decide for himself.

There is one vital and what may prove a deciding factor in favour of our soya meat bean produce. The average amount of protein which can be harvested from an acre of soya beans is nearly six times as much as that gained from an acre devoted to farming livestock.

This indeed is a comforting thought in times of inflation and ever increasing prices. Meat costs, together with all food prices, increase slowly but surely, and there is no hope that they are ever likely to come down again.

Soya bean farming in America is a relatively new crop – much has been learned about it, and more and better yields of beans are being produced. There is no question but that further improvements will follow. In many areas the Giant Yellow Mammoth bean has been replaced with a bean known as the Lee Soya Bean — this is said to be almost immune from disease and other setbacks. So progress continues in this new and fascinating industry.

Today, at least nineteen countries cultivate soya bean crops.

Summary

There is little doubt that a far greater world acreage of the soya bean could be cultivated. Such countries as Australia, New Zealand, and many parts of Africa have ideal climates.

Canada took a great interest in the crop, together with America, and carried out experiments and planting of species as far back as 1936. However, the Canadian Government do not seem to have made great progress. Possibly some parts of Canada are too far North for the crop to be grown.

As mentioned previously in this book there is a tendency to overproduce the bean in America. Farmers receive a subsidy from the American government for growing the bean.

Soya Oil

In the U.S.A. and many other countries soya oil has been accepted for a long time. The bulk of the oil used in margarine shortening, salad and cooking oils is soya oil. It is of excellent food value being rich in lecithin. The big problem, of course, is for producers to try and obtain like results with the protein content of the bean.

No problem will exist here for vegetarians or sections of the world's community who for religious or other reasons abstain from, or curtail their intake of animal flesh. All that is necessary is to bring knowledge of the bean and the soya protein foods to them and show how vital they are to fill gaps in meatless diets.

Soya Protein

When the demand for soya protein becomes as great as that for the oil the full benefits of this wonder crop will be available to man everywhere. For various reasons nowadays more people than ever are wondering if a daily intake of animal flesh is so vital to health. Meat is becoming increasingly more expensive to buy. Carcases of animals are found to contain greater amounts of DDT, and antibiotics are increasingly used to treat livestock. All these facts cause some people to purchase less meats.

Soya Milk: Milk Without Cows

For over 5,000 years this health-giving soya milk was part of the food of the ancient Chinese and other Eastern races. It is made up of an emulsion of soya beans in water. In 1959 The World Health Organization constructed a 1,000,000 dollar soya milk plant in Indonesia. Many million bottles of this milk are produced yearly by K. S. Lo. of Hong Kong. Very nutritious and cheaper than cow's milk, it has helped many of the unfortunate people in the East to survive. In the Western world soya milk has also been used to combat malnutrition or for persons allergic to cow's milk.

Grave Problem of the Future

The entire world animal agriculture is faced with a tremendous task. A formidable task indeed. This is where the little soya bean and all the amazing soya protein foods will prove more than a godsend – the difference for millions between enough to eat and star-

vation. This becomes apparent when I again quote:
'The average amount of protein which can be harvested from an acre of soya beans, is nearly six times as much as that gained from an acre devoted to farming livestock'.

The Hunzas

Is a daily intake of meat necessary for health? Obviously vegetarians and other non-meat eaters will say that it is not. One remarkable race of people exist on a practically meatless diet and live long useful lives to a great age, free from many diseases. These are the Hunzas who occupy a fertile valley, one hundred miles in length in West Pakistan.

Fifty years ago a Dr Robert McCarrison, Director of Nutritional Research in India, spent seven years with the Hunzas. In the book which he subsequently wrote Dr McCarrison has this to say about them: 'A race unsurpassed in perfection of physique and in freedom from disease. Amongst these people the span of life is extraordinarily long.'

An American, Rene Taylor, is one of the most recent writers to visit the Hunzas. Her book, *Long Suppressed Hunza Health Secrets* became a best seller. She met Hunza men and women enjoying robust physical and mental health at one hundred years of age and over.

It is accepted that Hunza men of ninety and one hundred years of age can father children. She saw people of eighty and ninety in a perfect state of health who had every appearance of being in their forties. Cancer, heart disease, and other serious complaints, accepted as unavoidable in western countries were practically unknown among the Hunzas.

Diet of the Hunzas

Naturally there are many factors which contribute towards the long lives and robust health of these people. Their relaxed way of life is free from the stresses and pressures of civilization, for they have no prisons, banks, money taxes, stores. There is no crime, no divorce and education is free to all.

They practise their own kind of Yoga, can walk for miles and lead strenuous outdoor lives. With all these aids to good health, even in the beautiful Hunza valley, in the long run what the people eat greatly determines what they become.

Let us take a look at the diet of the Hunzas in the 1960's, as Rene Taylor saw and wrote about in her book, one of the chapters of which is headed, 'The Amazing Hunza Diet'. Food which has provided centuries of good health for these happy, carefree people consists of grains, including wheat, barley, buckwheat and small grains – only wholemeal, white bread is never eaten. They eat leafy vegetables, potatoes and other root crops.

Rene Taylor found that the soya bean played a vital and important part in the Hunza diet, providing protein for the making of cheese, milk, bakery foods, etc. She said they only ate meat on rare occasions such as holidays, weddings and so on. Among other vegetables, sprouted soya beans were very frequently consumed.

There must be a number of reasons for the amazing vitality and long lives of the Hunzas. Being almost vegetarians they might well be expected to experience some shortage of protein. Of course there is not the slightest indication that they suffer from any such deficiencies. The little soya bean consumed extensively by this healthy race of people without doubt plays a vital part in keeping them not only strong, healthy and free from disease, but puts them on their own as one of the fittest races in the world.

It seems obvious if more people become familiar with the soya bean, and accept it as part of their diet, greater cultivation will surely follow. Without doubt it is a crop of the future for the Atomic Age.

The world and its teeming millions are bound to feel the effects, in the years ahead if the cultivation of this vital food is not allowed to keep pace with the ever increasing population. America has done her share, and it is hoped that other countries, who are able to cultivate this remarkable vegetable will make every effort to do so.

CHAPTER NINE

SOYA BEAN RECIPES

Today, soya beans and foods derived from crops have become more acceptable than a decade ago when this book first appeared in print. Some recipes are as up to date as the expanding soya processing industries; others have been handed down through ancient Chinese history and are served much the same as they were thousands of years ago.

The soya crop has an enormous potential which is slowly being more fully utilized. It may come as a surprise to learn that this remarkable vegetable can now be used to play a part throughout a meal from the serving of soup to the final course which can be in the form of soya bean coffee.

Quite a number of books have appeared in recent years devoted entirely to soya bean recipes of which there are hundreds. Here, I can only introduce a limited number, though enough, I hope, to whet your appetite to try more. With soya flour we have an excellent food which, believe it or not, contains about twice the protein content of meat.

Growing Soya Bean Industries

Rapid development has taken place in the manufacture of many foods from American crops but as always fresh beans direct from the fields can be used as a green vegetable.

Today, milk from soya bean crops is more widely used and can be purchased in many countries. Other foods include, flour, ice cream, confectionery, breakfast cereals, soya protein foods which are also used as additives or binders in sausages, meat pies, cold meats and in tinned foods.

Dried Soya Beans

There are three important things to remember in order of priority. First, all dried beans must be soaked in water overnight and the remaining water discarded. Secondly, fresh water should be added and the beans given a long cooking period (this effectively destroys any trypsin inhibitor which is poisonous). The final essential is to ensure that seasoning such as tomatoes, garlic, onions, soya sauce, marmite or some form of stock is used in combination with the beans. This makes for an appetizing dish, and failure to observe this important point may well put you off making a second attempt at sampling the dried bean. No one can pretend that the dried soya bean is as delicious as many other beans; but, like many dishes, a lot depends on the cook. Even our popular canned varieties of beans are prepared with tomato sauce, onion, curry powder or some other appetizer.

There can be a risk involved in the consumption of any raw beans and the soya bean is no exception. To reiterate, the two simple precautions to be taken are (a) simply soak the beans overnight in water and (b) adequately boil them until tender.

Soya Sauce

Eastern meals are flavoured with what is called in Japan Shoyu sauce or Soy sauce in China. It is served at practically every meal, in the same way as we use condiments. Soup, fish, poultry, meat and vegetables are flavoured with it. Only a small amount of sauce should be used, otherwise it will blot out the entire meal. It is made from a mixture of soya beans, flour, salt, sugar and caramel, and has a pleasant and distinctive flavour.

Bottles of this sauce may be purchased at any delicatessen shop. It is certainly not worth the trouble or expense of trying to make the sauce yourself. A bottle will last quite a long time, even with daily use, for it is very strong and concentrated, only a few drops are needed at a time.

Tofu

Often known as dried bean curd, is another famous food from the bean. Cubes of this curd are used in eastern cooking. The beans are soaked in water for one to two days. They are then pounded together, and put into small moulds with brine, and boiled till they become hard. It is becoming popular in America, and interest is beginning to be shown in Britain.

Bean Sprouts

Soya bean recipes would not be complete without a description of the making of bean sprouts. They have always been extensively used in Japan and China, and are becoming increasingly popular in other countries. To produce sprouts, soak a cupful of beans in water for two to three days until such time as they have begun to sprout. Then place all the sprouted beans in a large jam jar and cover with a damp muslin cloth. The pot should be kept at a temperature of about 70°F/21°C. Twice a day the sprouting beans should be rinsed in fresh water, and in about a week the pot will have become crammed full of delicious crispy bean sprouts which are ready for eating. These vegetable sprouts can either be cooked or served as a salad after the roots have been removed.

Preparation of Bean Sprouts

The correct way of cooking bean sprouts is by Chow or stir frying (this means in a small amount of oil, prepared quickly, the sprouts being stirred in the oil whilst cooking). They can be prepared with all kinds of meat or poultry, or with other vegetable courses. All other ingredients should be cut to the same thickness as the sprouts. The sprouts must not be cooked too long otherwise their fine taste and vitamin rich content is spoilt. They should be tasty and crisp when served.

SOYA SOUP

½ cupful of soya flour
3 tablespoonsful vegetable margarine or oil
½ teaspoonful curry powder
½ teaspoonful herb or sea salt
1 cupful of hot water
2 tablespoonsful chopped parsley and chives
2 cupsful of stock
2 teaspoonsful brown sugar
2 teaspoonsful soya sauce

Add soya flour to vegetable oil or melted margarine in a saucepan and cook for three minutes stirring constantly, add the hot water and allow to simmer until thick. Add the broth and allow to simmer, adding the curry powder, parsley and chives. A cupful of cooked mixed vegetables may be added, if desired. Serve hot with croutons for two or three persons.

Soya Bean Curd (Tofu)

A nutritious tasty dish in which fresh soya beans are used. If these are unavailable dried beans may be used and left in soak overnight.

½ to 1 lb (225–450g) fresh soya beans (or dried as the case may be) a little milk, yeast and salt.

After overnight soaking cook the beans in water without salt. When nearly cooked take off most of the water. Continue the cooking for a while till the skins are tender. Empty contents out into basin (earthenware) and leave overnight. This will allow the contents to become jellied. Reheat and drain off the rest of the liquid. Pass all the beans through a fine sieve. Add to the *purée* the drained off liquid. Add a little milk and some yeast to produce fermentation and salt to taste. Divide into squares of sizes required and leave them to 'take' when they are ready for eating.

BEAN CURD WITH FISH
This makes a very fine fish dish.

peanut or soya oil	soya sauce
bean curd (Tofu) and fish	spring onion
1 glass of sherry with a little green ginger	salt

Fry the piece of fish (whole) over a low flame until it is brown on both sides. Pour over the sherry and ginger mixture. Add a tablespoonful of soya sauce and chopped spring onion, salt to taste. Cook for a further 15 minutes and add the bean curd. Serve hot as soon as fish and curd are cooked.

SAVOURY SOYA BEANS

1 cupful of diced celery	½ medium-sized chopped onion
2 tablespoonsful diced green pepper	¼ cupful of lemon juice
3 cupsful of cooked soya beans	3 tablespoonsful soya lecithin spread
3 tomatoes (skinned and pulped)	½ cupful of breadcrumbs (wholemeal)
2 teaspoonsful sweet basil	½ teaspoonful sea or herb salt
a little soya or vegetable oil	

Sauté celery, onion and pepper in the oil. Add the basil and tomato allowing it to simmer for 30 minutes. Place the mixture of vegetable, celery, onions and pepper into a baking dish in alternate layers with the soya beans. Cover surface with breadcrumbs putting a little more vegetable oil or margarine on top. Bake in a moderate oven for about an hour, or until the top turns brown.

Salads

Dried beans after being soaked and cooked, or the green and tinned varieties, may all be served in salads, just like ordinary green or baked beans. The cook may use any combination desired, with lettuce, beetroot, celery, tomatoes, cucumber, watercress, onions, chives, green pepper and so on. The salad can be one of cheese, corned beef, salmon, egg or any other food that usually accompanies a salad.

SOYA BEAN MEAT ROLL

1½ cupsful soya beans
⅛ cupful soya sauce
¼ cupful peanut butter
1 teaspoonful cornstarch
2 teaspoonsful salt (herb or sea)
⅓ cupful cold water

Wash and soak beans. Drain off water and grind up the beans as thoroughly as possible by using an electric coffee grinder. Mix the beans carefully with all the other ingredients. Pour the mixture into a covered container and simmer or steam for about three hours. On cooling, the finished dish may be treated as a meat roll which can be sliced, broiled or served with gravy. If you do not possess an electric grinder, use the finest blade of a food chopper.

SOYA BEAN CUTLETS

1 cupful of any kind of cooked meat
1 egg
3 tablespoonsful soya or vegetable oil
breadcrumbs
salt (sea or herb to taste)
1½ cupsful of cooked soya beans
1 medium-sized onion
1 cupful mashed potatoes
flour

Cut the onion as finely as possible, dice the meat and

mash the cooked soya beans. Fry the meat together with the onion in oil for three minutes. Stir in the mashed potatoes and the beaten egg and season to taste. Put the contents on a breadboard and, after shaping, divide off into cutlets. Sprinkle the breadcrumbs and flour on each cutlet which is then fried in the soya or vegetable oil till brown.

Soya Flour

You can enhance, increase the food value, and make any vegetable or meat soup far more nutritious by using a proportion of soya flour. This is quite simply accomplished by adding one sixteenth of the quantity in soya flour. If, for example, you were preparing the equivalent of sixteen cups of soup then you would add one cup of soya flour to fifteen cups of soup. This is done by mixing the soya flour to an equal amount of the soup and adding this mixture to the soup in the pan a few minutes before cooking is complete.

The main thing to remember when using any form of soya product is that they have all been derived from a natural source and contain lots of nutritional elements. Both soya flour and milk are quite nutritious so only relatively small amounts need be used. This is especially important in the case of soya flour which must accompany ordinary flour and cannot be used for baking on its own.

Soya Sandwich Spreads

It is quite a simple matter to include soya flour in almost any sandwich spread to enhance the taste and bring so much more nourishment. The soya flour is just blended with any other ingredients. You may choose nuts, grains, peanut butter, apples, egg, cheese and so on. Here are two:

CHEESE SPREAD

For every three ounces of creamed cheese mix half a cupful of soya flour and two tablespoonsful of chopped parsley and a small chopped onion together with two tablespoonsful of salad dressing.

PEANUT SPREAD

Take half a cupful of soya flour and the same amounts of peanut butter and salad dressing and mix them all thoroughly together.